THE FOURTH LITTLE PIG

First Steck-Vaughn Edition 1992

Copyright © 1990 American Teacher Publications

Published by Steck-Vaughn Company

Library of Congress number: 90-8059

Library of Congress Cataloging in Publication Data.

Celsi, Teresa Noel.
  The fourth little pig / by Teresa Celsi; illustrated by Doug Cushman.

  (Ready-set-read)
  Summary: The sister of the Three Little Pigs comes to visit and tries to persuade her brothers, who have been hermits since an episode with a wolf, to overcome their fears and go outside.
  [1. Brothers and sisters—Fiction. 2. Fear—Fiction. 3. Pigs—Fiction. 4. Stories in rhyme.]
I. Cushman, Doug, ill. II. Title. III. Series.
PZ8.3.C34Fo [E]—dc20   1990   90-8059

ISBN 0-8172-3577-9   hardcover library binding

ISBN 0-8114-6740-6   softcover binding

        8 9   96 95 94 93

The Fourth Little Pig

by Teresa Celsi

illustrated by Doug Cushman

RSVP

**RAINTREE
STECK-VAUGHN**
P U B L I S H E R S
The Steck-Vaughn Company

Austin, Texas

With homes made of bricks
And of straw and of twigs.

5

Pig One and Pig Two
Then needed to flee,
So they ran off to stay
At the house of Pig Three.

7

They bolted the windows
And locked the front door.
"We won't go outside," they said.
"Not anymore."

They stayed in that house
At the top of a hill,

And those three silly pigs
Would be hiding there still—

If their sister, the bold and the daring Pig Four,
Hadn't stopped by to visit and knocked on their door.

"Go away, wolf," she heard. "Get away from our door!"
"I'm no wolf," she replied. "I'm your sister, Pig Four."

The door opened a crack, then it opened up wide.
"Get in," said the boys. "There are bad wolves outside."

"Oh, pooh," said Pig Four,
"There are no wolves in sight."
"Yes, there are!" said her brothers,
And they slammed the door tight.

"Keep still," said the brothers.
"Now everyone hide!"
"Why hide?" said their sister.
"You should all go outside."

"You can't spend your whole life
Just sitting and shaking.
There are places to see
And things to be making."

"You can build a canoe
Or go out and buy fudge."
But despite her suggestions,
The boys would not budge.

"Keep that door shut!"
The three brothers cried.
"We're safe in here, Sister.
We won't go outside."

15

"You're hopeless!" their sister
Cried out with a frown.
Then she huffed and she puffed
And she blew their house down!

As soon as the dust
Had started to clear,
Pig Four said, "You see,
There are no wolves out here."

The boys peeked over
What was left of their wall.
There were no wolves in sight—
There were no wolves at all!

"Hooray!" cried the brothers.
"How happy are we!
For the wolves are all gone,
And now we are free."

"We won't spend our whole lives
Just sitting and shaking.
There are places to see
And things to be making!"

21

The boys got some fudge, then they built a canoe.
Then they climbed up a mountain, enjoying the view.

FUDGE

And as for their sister, the daring Pig Four,
She traveled. She knows there are worlds to explore,
If only you're willing to open the door.

Sharing the Joy of Reading

Reading a book aloud to your child is just one way you can help your child experience the joy of reading. Now that you and your child have shared **The Fourth Little Pig,** you can help your child begin to think and react as a reader by encouraging him or her to:

- Retell or reread the story with you, looking and listening for the repetition of specific letters, sounds, words, or phrases.

- Make a picture of a favorite character, event, or key concept from this book.

- Talk about his or her own ideas or feelings about the characters in this book and other things that the characters might do.

Here is an activity that you can do together to help extend your child's appreciation of this book: You and your child can build your own version of a house for the little pigs. Use materials like shoe boxes, construction paper, and small wooden sticks. Once the house is built, you may wish to make three or four little pigs from cardboard who will "live" and "play" in the house.